Charlie
the Bridesmaid

Narinder Dhami
Illustrated by Jan Lewis

RIGBY

Chapter 1

Charlie was in the garden, playing
basketball by herself. Her jeans were
muddy, but Charlie didn't care. She
didn't mind getting dirty.

Charlie ran up to the basket, and was just about to shoot when her mother called her.

"Charlie! I've got a surprise for you!"

Charlie was excited.

"Great! I wonder what it is," she thought, as she ran into the house.

3

There was a large, white box lying on the table. Charlie got even more excited when she saw it. She never got packages in the post.

"The bridal shop sent it," said Charlie's mother. "It's your bridesmaid's dress!"

"Oh." Charlie's face fell. She really didn't want to be a bridesmaid at her aunt's wedding.

"Go on, open it," said her mother.

Charlie looked inside the box and felt sick. The dress was purple, and it had frills all over it.

"It's . . . *it's horrible!*" she gasped.

"Nonsense! It's lovely!" said her mother. "Now put it on and let's see how it looks."

Charlie made a face.

"Come on Charlie," said her mother.
"No arguments, please."

Charlie went to her room, and
came down with the dress on.
She felt really stupid in it.

"There! You look so pretty!"
said her mother.

"I look stupid!" Charlie
said, "I'm not wearing it!
No way!"

Her mother frowned. "What will Aunt Beth say?"

"I don't care!" Charlie yelled, as she pulled the dress off. "I hate it!"

"We'll talk about this later," said her mother, sharply. "Now take it up to your bedroom."

Charlie grabbed the bridesmaid's dress, and stormed out of the room. Why couldn't she wear her jeans to Aunt Beth's wedding instead of a silly dress?

Charlie was so angry, she wasn't looking
where she was going. She tripped over a
big plastic bag, which was lying in the hall.
The bag was full of clothes.

Charlie's mother had sorted them out
for a jumble sale that afternoon.

Suddenly Charlie had an idea. She pushed
the dress into the bag, underneath all the
other clothes, and ran upstairs.

Then Charlie's father came in, picked up
the bag, and carried it out to the car.
He drove off with the bag to the sale.

Charlie felt very pleased with herself.
Now she'd never see that horrible
dress again!

Later that day Aunt Beth came over.

"Hello, Charlie," she said, giving her
a hug. "This is for you."

And she gave Charlie
a great new CD.

"Thanks Aunt Beth!" Charlie said.
Her aunt always brought her a present
whenever she came to visit.

"Did you like your bridesmaid's dress?"
Aunt Beth asked her.

Charlie blushed. "Oh, yes."

"Good." Her aunt smiled. "You'll be a
beautiful bridesmaid!"

Charlie didn't know what to say.

"I can't wait for the wedding,"
said Aunt Beth. "It's going
to be a wonderful day!"

Chapter 2

Charlie began to feel rather guilty about the dress. Aunt Beth would be very upset when she found out what Charlie had done. The wedding day wouldn't be so wonderful after all.

"Charlie, I'm going to the jumble sale," called her mother. "Do you want to come?"

"Yes, please!" Charlie said quickly.

She had to try and get that dress back!

When Charlie and her mother arrived at the sale, there were lots of other people waiting to go in. Charlie was very worried. What if someone bought the bridesmaid's dress before she could get it back? Then everyone would find out what she'd done!

Jumble
Sale
Today!
opening
3pm

The sale began. There were lots of different stalls. Charlie ran around them all as fast as she could, but she couldn't see her dress. Maybe someone had already bought it!

Bric-

brac

17

Then she saw it! The dress was hanging
on a rack with lots of other clothes, and a
woman was looking through them.

Suddenly Charlie saw her pick the
bridesmaid's dress out!

"How pretty. I'll take this," said the woman
to the man behind the table.

"That's mine!" Charlie gasped.

The woman looked surprised. "No, it isn't!
I saw it first!"

"Oh, please can I have it?" Charlie begged.

"If it's yours, why is it for sale?" asked
the woman.

Charlie explained and the woman began to laugh.

"Well, I think you need it more than I do!" she said, and she gave Charlie the dress.

"Do you want to buy that?" the man asked Charlie.

"Yes, but I haven't got any money!" Charlie said.

"No money, no dress!" the man said.

He tried to pull the dress out of Charlie's hands, but Charlie wouldn't let go.

She had to get that dress back!

21

22

"I'll buy it for you," the woman said kindly, and she paid the man.

"Oh, thank you!" Charlie said gratefully.

"I hope you enjoy your aunt's wedding!" said the woman with a smile.

Aunt Beth's wedding was a wonderful day.
Everyone said Charlie looked lovely in her
bridesmaid's dress.

But there was something they didn't know . . .